Max the City Dog

A DAY AT THE BEACH

I am a Cavalier King Charles Spaniel, and I live in Brooklyn with my "people" family Joey, Cece and Ryan.

But I'm not fancy. I'm just plain "Max the City Dog".

I have many stories to share with you, in particular that day at the beach last week.

A day that changed my life forever...

The day starts like many others...

The sun is rising outside my window...
It's a perfect day to go to the beach
if I can convince my people
to take us there.

When the squirrels see me coming... they all chatter, "Here comes the Sheriff!"

I love chasing them up the trees, but it's all just friendly sport.

We are really good friends.

I finally convince Cece and Ryan
to take Joey and me to the beach.

After lunch we all take the subway
to Brighton Beach, my favorite!

I love riding on the subway in the
summer because the air is very cool
from the air-conditioning.

Sometimes
I ride in my
travel bag...

We get off the subway, walk by the NY Aquarium

and stop in to see the colorful fish tanks.

Nathan's, on the Coney Island boardwalk, is our next stop before we reach the beach.

Can you believe that Nathan's has been in business for over 100 years?

I love their hotdogs!

Oh, and don't forget Luna Park, the amusement zone at Coney Island...

Dino's Wonder Wheel, the big ferris wheel is fun! The other rides are just too crazy.

I see my friend Robbi who lives in the neighborhood, walking along by the Luna Park entrance...

Hey Max, let's go say hello?

Next we walk down to the beach
to take in some rays.

A few minutes later, I am way too hot!
A good place to cool off is under the
Coney Island Pier.

It's time for us to go visit our lifeguard friends on the beach.

There's the main lifeguard and his buddy who are posted in the main Coney Island beach zone.

Joey and I go to the ocean's edge
to run in the waves crashing on the shore.

But then Joey dives under a big wave.
Uh, Oh...for a minute I can't see him at all!

I BARK and BARK and fantically run
up and down the beach...

The lifeguard sees me barking and races into the water...

He knows that a riptide is a strong current that can very quickly pull you out toward the sea.

The lifeguard is a strong swimmer
and reaches Joey quickly.

Joey is saved! I am so happy!

Everyone on the beach cheers
and calls me a HERO!

I feel good, knowing that I helped
save Joey's life.

Boy, was that an exciting afternoon!

Ryan and Cece put up our beach umbrella so we can all have another rest.

Joey and I are so happy to be safely back together again..

I have to be carried back home
on the subway...

I'm still very tired from
all the drama of the day!

Back home, it really feels good to sleep in my own bed. Can't wait for another adventure tomorrow?

CPSIA information can be obtained
at www.ICGtesting.com
Printed in the USA
LVHW070534141220
674086LV00039B/1588